Lexile: _AD 140L_

AR/BL: _0.8_

AR Points: _0.5_

JON SCIESZKA'S TRUCKTOWN
THE SPOOKY TIRE

WRITTEN BY JON SCIESZKA

CHARACTERS AND ENVIRONMENTS DEVELOPED BY THE

DAVID SHANNON   LOREN LONG   DAVID GORDON

ILLUSTRATION CREW:

Executive producer: Keytoon, Inc. in association with Animagic S.L.

Creative supervisor: Sergio Pablos ○ Drawings by: Juan Pablo Navas ○ Color by: Isabel Nadal

Color assistant: Gabriela Lazbal ○ Art director: Karin Paprocki

READY-TO-ROLL

ALADDIN

NEW YORK   LONDON   TORONTO   SYDNEY

ALADDIN PAPERBACKS

An imprint of Simon & Schuster Children's Publishing Division

1230 Avenue of the Americas, New York, NY 10020

Copyright © 2009 by JRS Worldwide, LLC.

All rights reserved, including the right of reproduction in whole or in part in any form.

READY-TO-READ, ALADDIN PAPERBACKS, and related logo
are registered trademarks of Simon & Schuster, Inc

TRUCKTOWN and JON SCIESZKA'S TRUCKTOWN and design are trademarks of JRS Worldwide, LLC.

The text of this book was set in Truck King.   Manufactured in the United States of America

First Aladdin Paperbacks edition August 2009   10 9 8 7 6 5 4 3 2 1

Library of Congress Cataloging-in-Publication Data

Scieszka, Jon.

The spooky tire / written by Jon Scieszka ; characters and environments developed by
the Design Garage: David Shannon, Loren Long, David Gordon.—1st Aladdin Paperbacks ed.

p. cm.—(Trucktown. Ready-to-roll)

"Illustration crew: Executive Producer: Keytoon in association with Animagic S.L., Creative Supervisor: Sergio Pablos.

Drawings by: Juan Pablo Navas, Color by: Isabel Nadal, Color Assistant: Gabriela Lazbal, Art Director: Karin Paprocki."

Summary: On a dark and stormy night, Melvin the truck rolls into a spooky junkyard to find a replacement for his flat tire.

ISBN: 978-1-4169-4142-2 (pbk)

ISBN: 978-1-4169-4153-8 (library)

[1. Trucks—Fiction. 2. Tires—Fiction. 3. Ghosts—Fiction] I. Design Garage. II. Shannon, David, ill.

III. Long, Loren, ill. IV. Gordon, David, 1965 Jan. 22— ill. V. Title.

PZ7.S41267Sp 2009

[E]—dc22

2007027776

It was dark.
It was stormy.
It was night.

Melvin had a **flat** tire.

Melvin rolled into
a **spooky**
junkyard.

He found a new tire.

Melvin was worried.
Melvin was scared.

Melvin drove home
FAST!

Melvin parked.

Melvin hid.

"Who took my golden tire?"

The
spooky
voice
had
found
him!

Melvin closed

"Who took The voice

Ok
den

The voice was closer.

Something bumped
Melvin's house.

"Don't you want the other one?" asked Jack. But Melvin never heard him.